The Tale of Two Nuts

By Natasha Guruleva

To Janet

Cover and interior page design by Natasha Guruleva

Mother Oak

loved her acorn-kids. She took

care of them, making sure they

grew robust and shiny. After the

acorns fell down on the ground

she taught them how to root and

become the best trees they could

be. Year after year new acorns

rooted in the forest and

grew into new oaks.

One time she gave birth to Leafy and Branchy, the acorns. She taught them about the importance and honor of being trees. Mother Oak told them that trees create oxygen: without it life on Earth wouldn't be possible. She said that trees give food and refuge to many creatures of the world, and there is nothing more noble than being a tree, but Leafy and Branchy were not eager to follow the tradition.

They didn't want to root, but travel and learn about the world first. "You're truly nuts," scolded their Mother Oak after she got tired of all the kind and wise words trying to convince Leafy and Branchy to stay under her protection and do what the oaks were doing since the beginning of their time.

On one late summer day

Leafy and Branchy finally fell on the ground.

They didn't stay under the shade of their mother

even for a minute – the rebellious acorns

immediately took off along the path

in the forest.

Everything was new and exciting for them:
they saw the grass and beautiful flowers, they
marveled at butterflies and bugs. They left
the oak grove and now were surrounded by
different trees – the gorgeous
evergreen conifers.

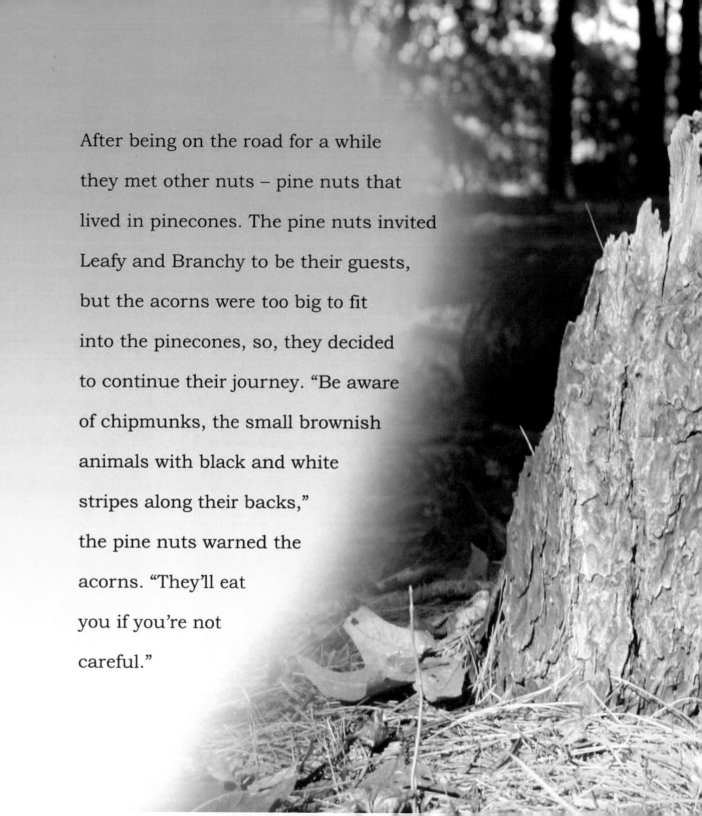

After being on the road for a while
they met other nuts – pine nuts that
lived in pinecones. The pine nuts invited
Leafy and Branchy to be their guests,
but the acorns were too big to fit
into the pinecones, so, they decided
to continue their journey. "Be aware
of chipmunks, the small brownish
animals with black and white
stripes along their backs,"
the pine nuts warned the
acorns. "They'll eat
you if you're not
careful."

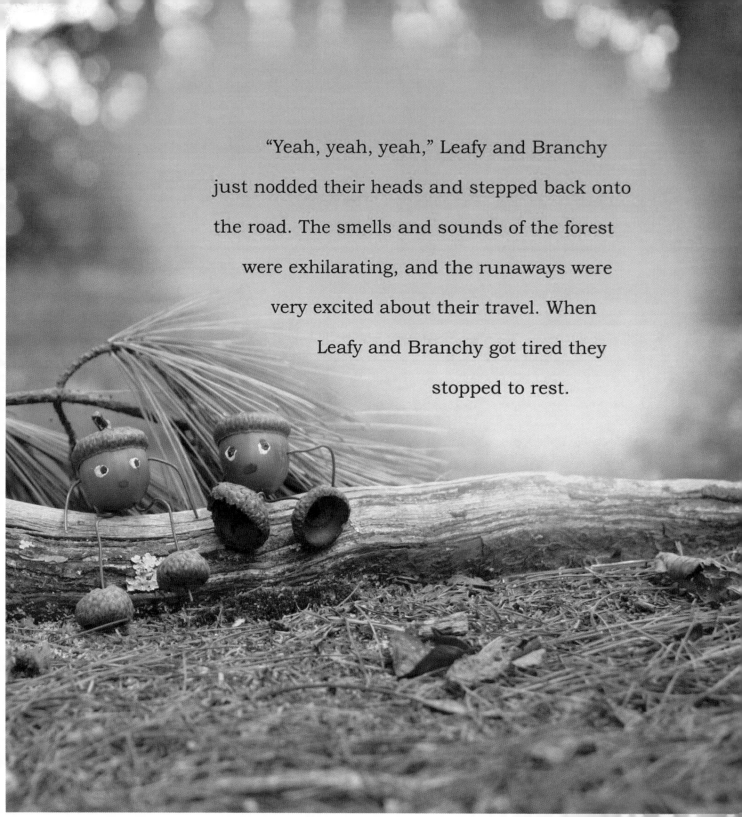

"Yeah, yeah, yeah," Leafy and Branchy
just nodded their heads and stepped back onto
the road. The smells and sounds of the forest
were exhilarating, and the runaways were
very excited about their travel. When
Leafy and Branchy got tired they
stopped to rest.

Suddenly they felt that they were under a scrutinizing glance
of the eyes of some animal. From the look of him they realized
that it was a chipmunk. They wanted to flee, but the chipmunk
was much faster than them – he caught the acorns, put them
behind his cheeks and brought them to his den.

Leafy and Branchy were very scared. Luckily for them the chipmunk wasn't hungry. He left them alone and went out to continue his hunt for rainy day provisions.

The acorns didn't want to become the chipmunk's food. They looked around, found their way out of the den and escaped.

The den was on the edge of a field where a few cows were grazing. Leafy and Branchy jumped onto one of the cows' tails, and thus were carried to the opposite edge of the field and then to the pond.

The nuts fell onto the grass and looked around: the pond seemed very beautiful and peaceful. They decided to embark on an unattached lily pad and do some sailing. The sun was blazing, the water was cool.

Suddenly they noticed a flock of birds. Evidently they were hungry and saw two acorns as an appetizer. Leafy and Branchy dove under the lily pad and hid there.

After the ducks left, the acorns decided that being sailors was not worth pursuing and landed on the other side of the pond. They were tired and disoriented. The acorns started missing their mother. They thought they learned a lot about the world and that maybe rooting was not such a bad idea after all, but they had no clue how to do it, and there were no oaks around to teach them.

Leafy and Branchy wandered and wandered until their little feet brought them to Forest Town where Mushroom people lived. The mushrooms were very kind to the nuts - they let the acorns rest and then advised them to seek Rootman: he was a wizard and knew many things – the mushrooms thought he could help Leafy and Branchy. So, they took the acorns to see the wizard.

Rootman was ancient – he looked like dry roots of an old tree. Without anything said he knew what Leafy and Branchy's problem was.

"Are you sure you truly want to root?" he asked.

"Yes, we traveled the world, we've met many beings and we think that there is nothing more noble than being a tree," they said with one voice.

"Alright, I believe you," responded Rootman, "but do you have some tree spirit left inside of you - because without it you are just food for animals. You were out of touch with your kind for so long..."

"We do have what it takes," Branchy assured Rootman for both of them. "Tell us what to do to prove it and we'll do it."

"Actually, you don't have to do anything," said Rootman. "I'll send you to your Mother Oak, and if you still have tree spirit, you'll get to her, but if not – you'll stay here with the mushrooms, they are not bad company, believe me."

With these words out of nowhere he produced two oak leaves, asked Leafy and Branchy to board them and blew real hard. The acorns didn't even notice how they were brought back where they had started – under the shade of their Mother Oak. She was so glad to see her offspring by her side once again.

It didn't take long for Leafy and Branchy to root – as they were ready for it. In a few years they became strong and beautiful oak trees. The birds made their nests on their branches, and many creatures enjoyed their shade. The mushrooms grew near their trunks and people were inspired to write poetry about them.

INTERESTING FACTS

Oak trees can live 200 or more years. The largest oak tree on record is *The Seven Sisters Oak* in Lewisburg, Mandeville, Louisiana. It measures 37 feet and 2 inches in circumference with a crown spread of 150 feet. It is estimated that it is more than 1,000 years old!

Oak trees can start producing acorns when they are 20 years old, but sometimes the first acorn production can start at the age of 50. By the time the tree is 70 to 80 years old it will produce thousands of acorns.

In a good year the oak tree will have many flowers - up to several thousand. With the right humidity, temperature, no late frost in the spring, and sufficient rainfall in the summer, tiny scale-covered acorns (called nubbins at that point) begin to grow. They will mature to become full grown and ripe acorns by late summer. The chances of one acorn making it to become an oak tree are very slim - less than 1/10,000. That means that for every 10,000 acorns, only one will become a tree!

There is a wise man named Rootman that lives in Florida. He helps many people.

www.mushroomland.net

Made in the USA
Charleston, SC
19 August 2010